Run in the Rainforest

AF605650

Written by Simon Cheshire
Illustrated by Sarah Horne

Ed and Lin were with their dad. He went to lots of places to take photos. This time they were in the rainforest in South America.

They got out of the boat. Lots of eyes watched them.

“It’s so noisy here!” Lin shouted.

“It’s like all the birds and animals are shouting at each other!” said Ed.

Dad was taking photos of some monkeys.

A flock of noisy birds flew past.
"Look at those parrots!" said Ed.
"Let's follow them."

“Stop!” said Lin. “I’m so hot.
I want to go for a swim.”

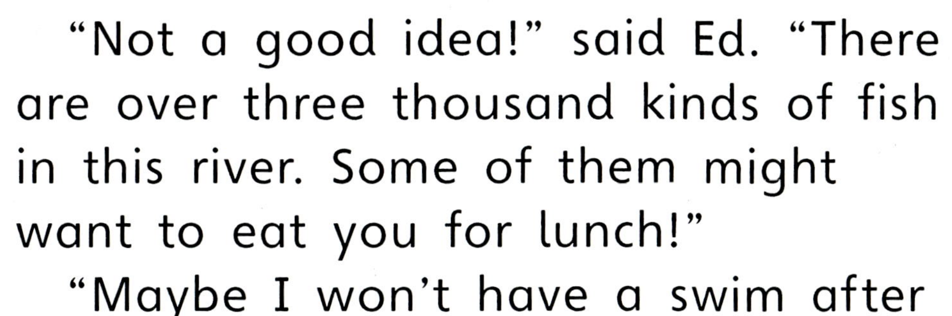

"Not a good idea!" said Ed. "There are over three thousand kinds of fish in this river. Some of them might want to eat you for lunch!"

"Maybe I won't have a swim after all," said Lin.

"I bet there are dangerous animals hiding in the bushes," said Ed. "They are just waiting to get us!"

Lin found a big stick. “I can fight off any dangerous animals with this!” she said.

Then Lin saw a big shape moving slowly behind a bush. "Ed," she said, "are there *really* big, dangerous animals in the rainforest?"

"Yes, lots! There is one called a jaguar," Ed said. "It's like a very big, scary cat. Why?"

jaguar

spotty fur

big teeth

sharp claws

"Um, I think there might be one behind that bush!" said Lin.
A large, spotted head popped up.

Aaargh!
Run!

Ed couldn't remember seeing photos of a jaguar quite like this one in the rainforest. This animal was huge... and it was coming after him.

Time to run!

The animal was quick.

Ed was quicker.

Lin was as quick as lightning!

Dad rushed after them.

Suddenly they were in a village. There were lots of people all dressed up. They were dancing and singing.

"Run!" Lin shouted to them. "A huge animal is right behind us. Don't let it get you!"

Everyone laughed. Lin and Ed looked at the villagers... and then looked to see what was so funny.

They saw the animal come out of the bushes. It was wearing shoes!

"Sorry if we scared you," said a boy. "We made this jaguar for our festival today."

"I kind of knew that it couldn't be a real ja... jag..." Lin said to him.
"Jaguar!" said Ed.
"See, *this* jaguar is friendly," said the boy. "Now, come and join in our festival."

Ed and me at the rainforest festival. We are the jaguar!